淘气的乒乓猫

乒乓猫大冒险

〔荷〕米斯·博豪宇斯 著　　〔荷〕菲珀·维斯顿多普 绘　　蒋佳惠 译

Fiep

人民文学出版社
PEOPLE'S LITERATURE PUBLISHING HOUSE

乒乒和乓乓舒舒服服地待在暖和的房间里，
望着外面飞舞的雪花。

**Pim and Pom are snuggled up inside
watching the snowflakes.**

"你看，乒乒，那儿有只年老的流浪猫。
他肯定很饿，一定觉得很冷。"

'Look Pom, there's that old stray cat.
He must be very hungry. And cold.'

"这样吧，"乒乓说，
"我们请他进来吃饭吧。"

'I've got an idea,' says Pom.
'Let's invite him for dinner.'

年老的流浪猫实在饿坏了！
他狼吞虎咽，把鱼吃了个精光。

The old stray cat is very hungry indeed.
He greedily eats the fish.

"你不想多待一会儿吗？" 乒乓问，
"屋里很舒服，很暖和。"

'Don't you want to stay a while?' asks Pom.
'It is nice and warm inside.'

"待在屋里？哈！屋子外面才有真正的生活！"
年老的流浪猫说。

'Inside? Huh! Real life is outside,'
says the old stray cat.

"真正的生活？外面？"
乒乒和乓乓好奇地问道。

'Real life? Outside?'
Pim and Pom ask curiously.

"要知道，外面有各种各样的奇遇。对我来说，屋子里面的生活太无聊了。
只有你们这些宠物猫才会喜欢。"

'Outside is where adventures happen. Inside is too boring for me.
Inside is for house cats like you.'

乒乒才不想做一只无聊的宠物猫呢，
他也想到外面去生活，去经历奇遇！

Pim doesn't want to be a boring house cat.
He also wants an outside life, with adventures!

"你去吗，乒乓？
要不然，我就自己去了。"

'Are you coming, Pom?
Otherwise I will go on my own.'

可是，乒乓当然不会对他的朋友不管不顾。

But Pom doesn't leave his friend of course.

他们两个像真正的流浪猫一样，
走进寒冷的冬夜。

**Like two real stray cats
they go into the cold winter's night.**

哈，那里有垃圾桶。

"想到垃圾桶里去找些好吃的吗，乒乓？"

Ha, there are garbage cans.
'Fancy a bite to eat from the rubbish-bin, Pom?'

兵兵一点儿也不喜欢。
可是，真正的流浪猫只能这么做。

Pom doesn't like eating from a rubbish-bin,
but that is what real stray cats have to do.

"嗯，我不介意吃些鱼。"
乒乓勇敢地说。

**'Mmm, I wouldn't mind some fish,'
says Pom bravely.**

乒乒和乒乓继续在城市里游荡。

Pim and Pom go on roaming the city.

"你听见了吗，乒乓？"

'Do you hear that, Pom?'

"真正的流浪猫！跟我来！"

'Real stray cats, come on!'

乒乒和乓乓开开心心地同流浪猫们一起唱起歌来。

喵……喵！

Pim and Pom sing cheerfully with the stray cats.

Miaaaaaaow!

"吵够了吗？安静点！"一个气呼呼的声音嚷嚷起来。
所有的猫咪四处逃散，只有乒乒和乓乓待在原地没有动弹。然后……

'Be Quiet! Stop the noise!' an angry voice shouts.
All the cats run away. Only Pim and Pom stay. And then...

整整一桶水浇在了他们身上！

They get an entire bucket of water thrown on them.

哎呀呀，这下他们从头到脚都湿透了！

Oh no, now they're all wet.

"当流浪猫很好玩吧，乒乒？"
"这是一场真正的奇遇，乒乒。"乒乒一边瑟瑟发抖，一边说。

'It's fun being a stray, eh Pom.'
'It's a real adventure, Pim,' says Pom shiveringly.

所有的宠物猫都舒舒服服地待在暖和的房间里。乒乒很想回家，
可是他总不能令乒乒失望吧？

**All the house cats are snuggled up inside. Pom would like to go home,
but he can't let Pim down, can he?**

"要当一只流浪猫，就要露宿街头，
乒乒，那是一种艰难的古老的生活方式，你懂的。"

**'Stray cats sleep outside, Pim,
A tough old life, you know.'**

"是啊，乒乓，冒着大雪度过一夜，
这才算得上真正的奇遇！"

'Yes, Pom, a real adventure,
one night in the snow.'

"快看，乒乓，
这里有一个空盒子，用它作窝很舒适。"

'Look Pim, this empty box
will make a cosy bed.'

"仔细想想，真正的流浪猫只能睡在人行道上。"

'On second thoughts the pavement
will have to do instead.'

"做个好梦，乒乒。""晚安，乓乓。"毫无疑问，他们冷冰冰、湿漉漉。
"那些睡在屋子里的宠物猫们实在是错失良机。"

'Night night Pim,' 'Sleep tight, Pom.' They're wet and cold, no doubt.
'Those house cats sleeping inside are really missing out.'

"乒乓，我睡不着，这个地面也太硬了。"

'Pom, I'm not asleep yet.
It's hard here on the ground.'

"乒乓，我听见了可怕的声音！
我们现在回家去好吗？"

'Pom, can we go home now please?
I heard a scary sound!'

乒乓表示完全同意。

"走吧，乒乓，回我们自己的窝吧。"

Pom totally agrees.
'Come on Pim, let's go back to our basket.'

"我们不再是流浪猫了吧，乒乒？"
"是的，乒乒，我们是真正的宠物猫。"

'Aren't we stray cats anymore, Pom?'
'No Pim, we're real house cats.'

乒乒和乓乓，我们的宠物猫，躺在自己温暖的窝里，
舒舒服服地睡着了。

There they are, our house cats.
Warm and cosy in their own basket.

睡个好觉，乒乒和乓乓！

Sleep tight, Pim and Pom!